T0379084

PARANORMAL TECH

Searching for Aliens with Tech

by Megan Cooley Peterson

CAPSTONE PRESS
a capstone imprint

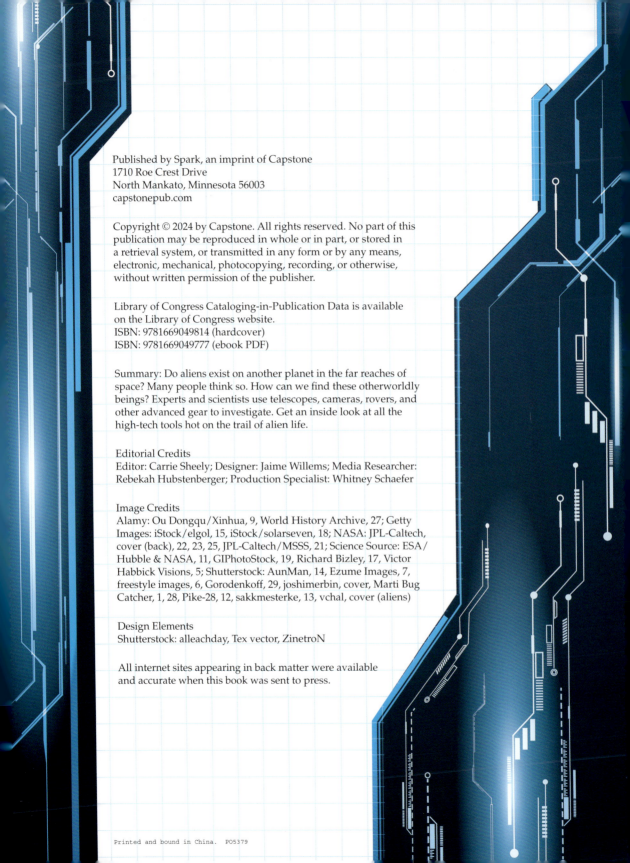

Published by Spark, an imprint of Capstone
1710 Roe Crest Drive
North Mankato, Minnesota 56003
capstonepub.com

Copyright © 2024 by Capstone. All rights reserved. No part of this publication may be reproduced in whole or in part, or stored in a retrieval system, or transmitted in any form or by any means, electronic, mechanical, photocopying, recording, or otherwise, without written permission of the publisher.

Library of Congress Cataloging-in-Publication Data is available on the Library of Congress website.
ISBN: 9781669049814 (hardcover)
ISBN: 9781669049777 (ebook PDF)

Summary: Do aliens exist on another planet in the far reaches of space? Many people think so. How can we find these otherworldly beings? Experts and scientists use telescopes, cameras, rovers, and other advanced gear to investigate. Get an inside look at all the high-tech tools hot on the trail of alien life.

Editorial Credits
Editor: Carrie Sheely; Designer: Jaime Willems; Media Researcher: Rebekah Hubstenberger; Production Specialist: Whitney Schaefer

Image Credits
Alamy: Ou Dongqu/Xinhua, 9, World History Archive, 27; Getty Images: iStock/elgol, 15, iStock/solarseven, 18; NASA: JPL-Caltech, cover (back), 22, 23, 25, JPL-Caltech/MSSS, 21; Science Source: ESA/Hubble & NASA, 11, GIPhotoStock, 19, Richard Bizley, 17, Victor Habbick Visions, 5; Shutterstock: AunMan, 14, Ezume Images, 7, freestyle images, 6, Gorodenkoff, 29, joshimerbin, cover, Marti Bug Catcher, 1, 28, Pike-28, 12, sakkmesterke, 13, vchal, cover (aliens)

Design Elements
Shutterstock: alleachday, Tex vector, ZinetroN

All internet sites appearing in back matter were available and accurate when this book was sent to press.

Printed and bound in China. PO5379

Table of Contents

Are Aliens Real? 4

Searching Outer Space 6

Looking for Laser Light 16

Blasting Off 20

Finding Aliens on Earth 26

    Glossary 30

    Read More 31

    Internet Sites 31

    Index 32

    About the Author 32

Words in **bold** are in the glossary.

Are Aliens Real?

Earth. It's the perfect home for us. But what about the rest of the **universe**? Could aliens live somewhere in space? If so, what would they be like?

To find out, first we have to find them. So far, no one has found **proof** that aliens are real. But new **technology** could change that. Scientists use the latest tools to look for aliens. What might they find?

Searching Outer Space

If aliens are real, they might have better spacecraft and tech than us. Scientists think alien tech might leave behind light, sound, or heat. They use tools to search for these signs of alien life.

Searching space is a big job. It needs big tools. Scientists use huge radio **telescopes**. They look for radio waves in space. Radio waves are a kind of **energy**. They can travel long distances. People can't see them. But radio telescopes can.

Fact

The biggest single-dish radio telescope is in China. Known as the FAST telescope, it's more than 1,600 feet (485 meters) wide.

In December 2020, a telescope picked up radio waves. They came from a star called Proxima Centauri. Two **planets orbit** this star. Did aliens from these planets make the radio waves?

Fact

Proxima Centauri is Earth's closest star other than the sun.

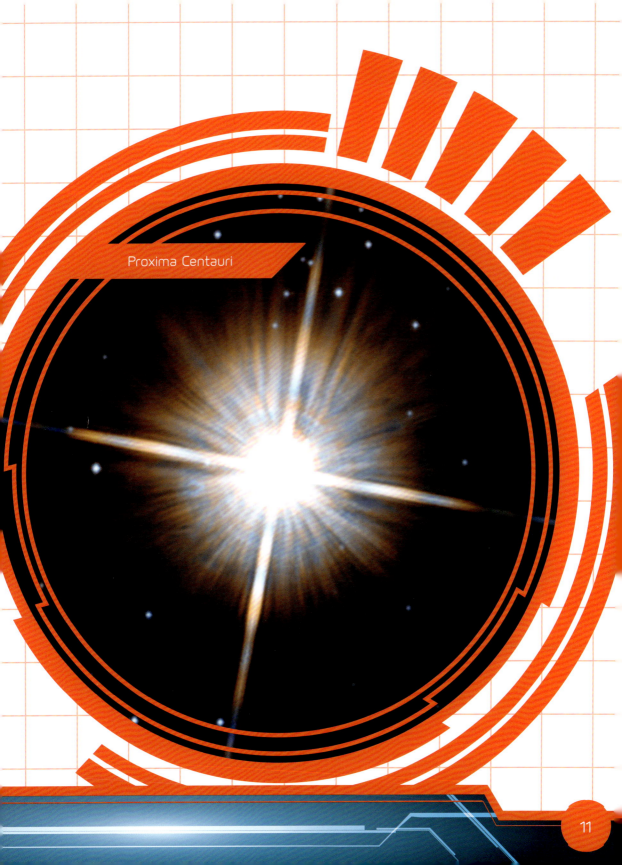
Proxima Centauri

Sagitarrius

Sagittarius is a group of stars. In 1977, a radio signal came from these stars. It was the strongest ever found in space. Some scientists say a **comet** made the signal. But others think aliens could have made it.

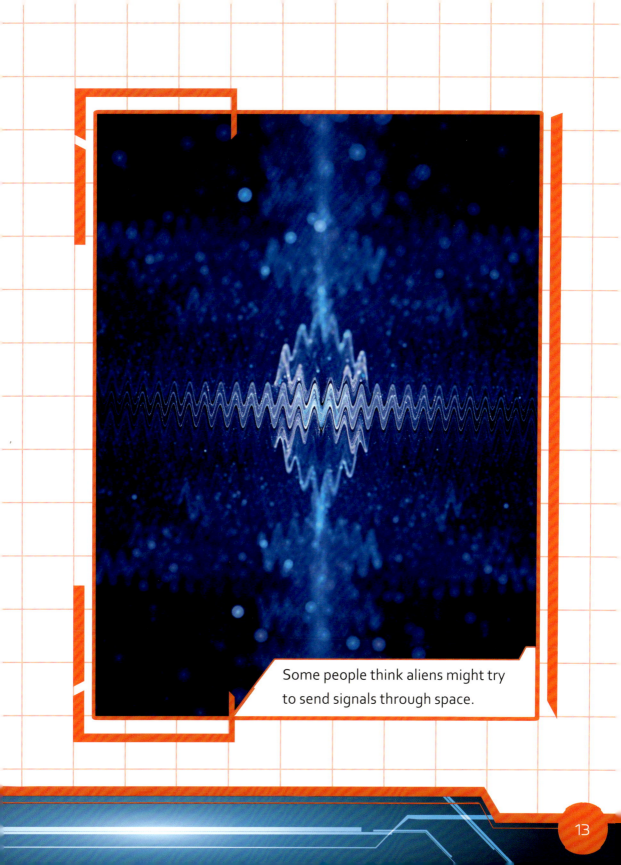

Some people think aliens might try to send signals through space.

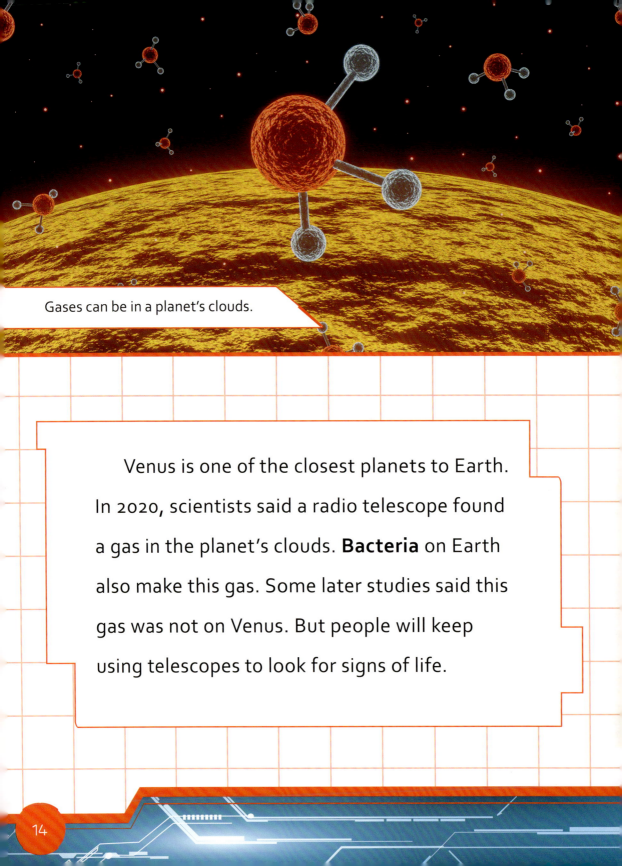

Gases can be in a planet's clouds.

Venus is one of the closest planets to Earth. In 2020, scientists said a radio telescope found a gas in the planet's clouds. **Bacteria** on Earth also make this gas. Some later studies said this gas was not on Venus. But people will keep using telescopes to look for signs of life.

Fact

The James Clerk Maxwell Telescope in Hawaii sees objects far out in space. It can find gases.

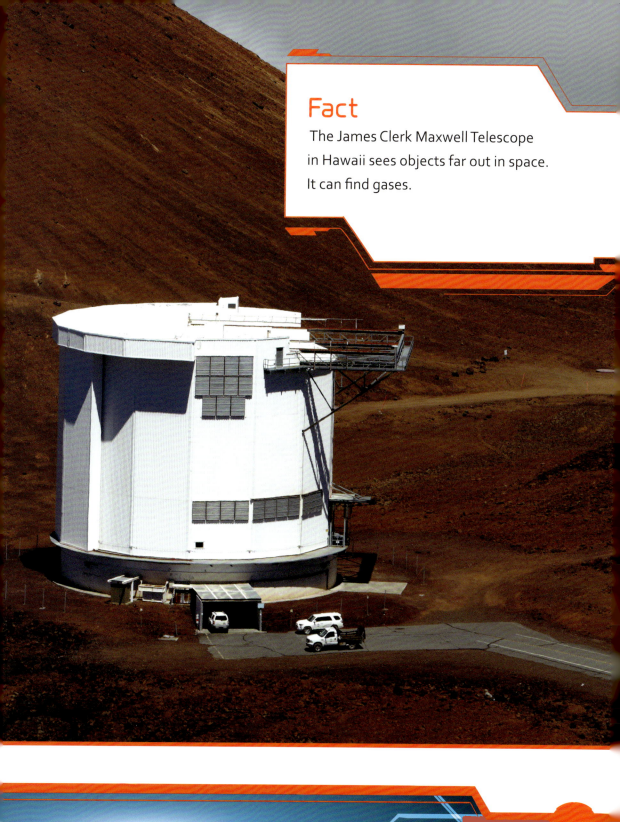

Looking for Laser Light

On Earth, people send text messages to friends. Could aliens send messages using **lasers**? Some scientists think they might. Laser light can send more information faster than radio waves. Laser light might also help push alien crafts through space.

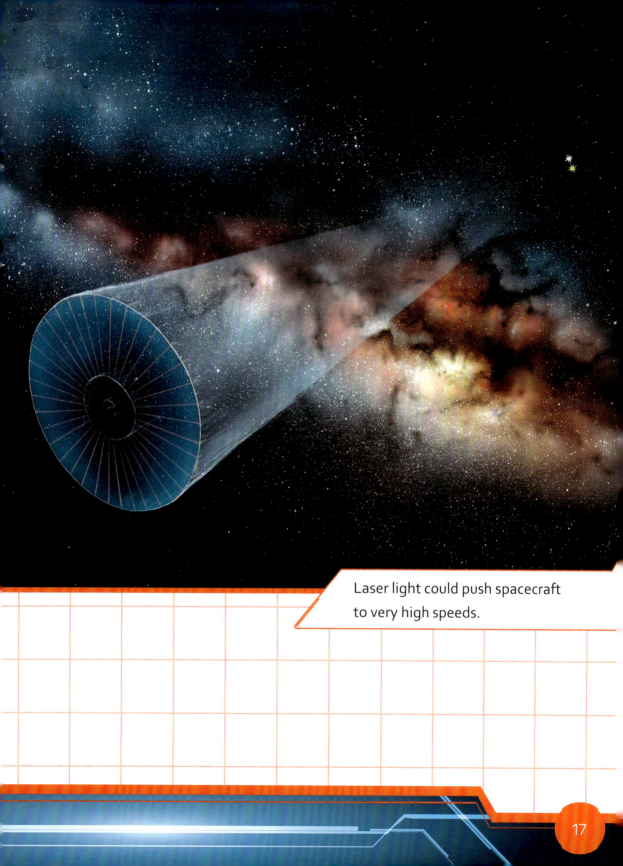

Laser light could push spacecraft to very high speeds.

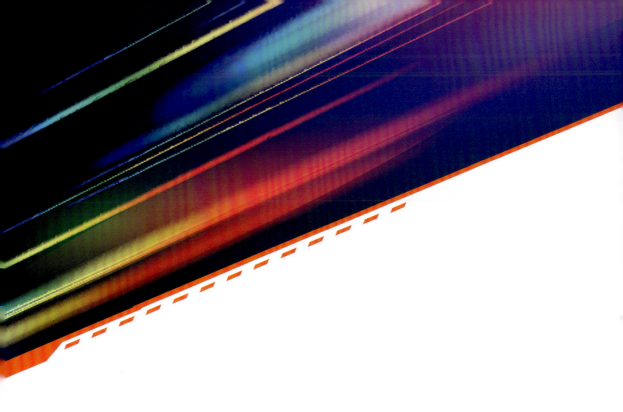

Scientists use high-tech cameras to find laser flashes. How? The camera breaks up the light. Starlight becomes a rainbow of colors. But laser light stays only a single color. These cameras can tell the difference between laser light and starlight.

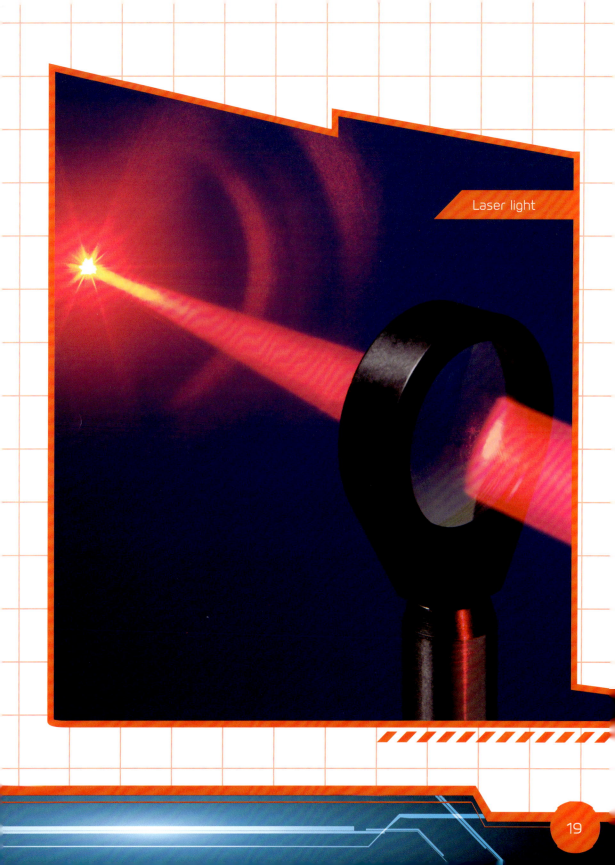
Laser light

Blasting Off

If aliens are real, they might never come to Earth. Scientists send spacecraft to other planets. They hope to find alien life there.

The U.S. space agency, NASA, sent the Curiosity **rover** to Mars. It got there in 2012. It found carbon. Carbon is found in living things on Earth. This could mean there was once life on Mars.

Curiosity

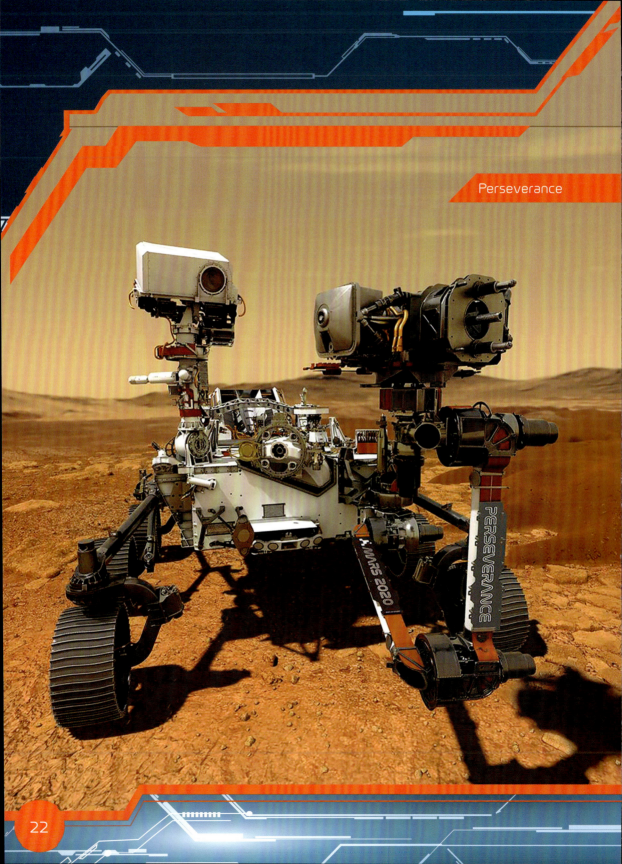
Perseverance

Water was once on Mars. Water can be a sign that this planet had life. NASA's Perseverance rover landed on Mars in 2021. The rover collects rocks at Jezero Crater. This crater used to be a lake. The rocks will return to Earth by 2033. Proof of alien life could be inside these rocks.

Jezero Crater as it may have looked billions of years ago

The planet Jupiter has many moons. Scientists think the moon Europa has water trapped under ice. NASA plans to send the Europa Clipper spacecraft to orbit Jupiter in 2024. It will take a close look at the moon. One day, a craft could tunnel through the ice. It could search the water for signs of life.

Fact
Europa may have twice as much water as Earth.

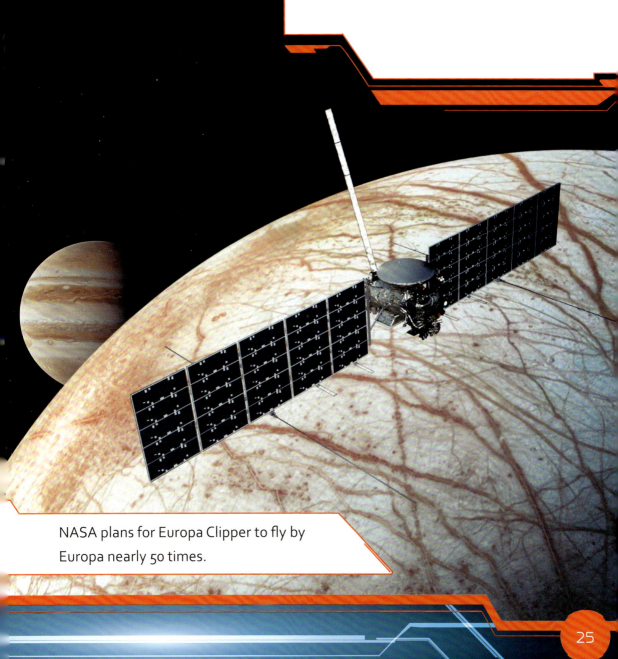

NASA plans for Europa Clipper to fly by Europa nearly 50 times.

Finding Aliens on Earth

What if aliens are already on Earth? Can tech find them? In 1961, Barney and Betty Hill said aliens took them. Betty later found pink powder on her dress. Scientists tested it using a tool. It can find out what something is made of using light. But the test gave them no answers. No one knows what made up the powder.

Betty and Barney Hill

Some people say they've seen aliens on Earth. A machine called a **polygraph** can put these stories to the test. A person is hooked up to the machine. They answer questions.

If the person is lying, they might breathe faster. Their heart might beat faster. The machine senses these changes. Does passing this test mean aliens could be real? You decide.

A person takes a lie detector test.

Glossary

bacteria (bak-TEER-ee-uh)—very small living things that exist all around you and inside you; some bacteria cause disease

comet (KOM-uht)—a ball of rock and ice that circles the sun

energy (E-nuhr-jee)—the ability to do work, such as moving things or giving heat or light

laser (LAY-zur)—equipment that makes thin, powerful beams of light

orbit (OR-bit)—to travel around an object in space

planet (PLAN-it)—a large object that moves around a star; Earth is a planet

polygraph (PAH-lee-graf)—a machine used to help find out if someone is telling the truth

proof (PROOF)—facts or evidence that something is true

rover (ROH-vur)—a small vehicle that people can move by using remote control; rovers are used to explore objects in space

technology (tek-NOL-uh-jee)—the use of science to do practical things, such as designing complex machines

telescope (TEL-uh-skope)—an instrument made of lenses and mirrors that is used to view distant objects

universe (YOO-nuh-verss)—everything that exists, including the earth, the planets, the stars, and all of space

Read More

Finn, Peter. *Do Aliens Exist?* New York: Gareth Stevens Publishing, 2022.

Olson, Gillia M. *Curious About Aliens.* Mankato, MN: Amicus, 2022.

Spilsbury, Louise. *Alien Visitations.* New York: Crabtree Publishing, 2022.

Internet Sites

Kiddle: Extraterrestrial Life Facts for Kids
kids.kiddle.co/Extraterrestrial_life

Kid Scoop.com: Are Aliens Real?
kidscoop.com/this-week-in-kid-scoop/are-aliens-real/

NASA Kids' Club
nasa.gov/kidsclub/index.html

Index

bacteria, 14

cameras, 18
carbon, 20
comets, 12

Europa, 24, 25

gases, 14, 15

Hill, Barney, 26
Hill, Betty, 26

Jezero Crater, 23

lasers, 16, 17, 18
light, 7, 16, 17, 18, 19

NASA, 20, 23, 24

planets, 10, 14, 20, 23, 24
  Jupiter, 24, 25
  Mars, 20, 23
  Venus, 14
polygraphs, 29
powder, 26

radio waves, 8, 10, 16
rovers, 20, 23

stars, 10, 12

telescopes, 8, 9, 10, 14, 15

water, 23, 24, 25

About the Author

Megan Cooley Peterson is a writer, editor, and bookworm. When she isn't writing or reading, you can find her watching movies or planning her next Halloween party. She lives in Minnesota with her husband and daughter.